For my parents, the bravest people I know. And
for Hamilton, my best friend and biggest supporter.
—APK

For Hien. I'll always be your mama,
and you'll always be my love.
—TB

Finding Papa
Text copyright © 2023 by Angela Pham Krans
Illustrations copyright © 2023 by Thi Bui
All rights reserved. Manufactured in Italy.
No part of this book may be used or reproduced in any manner whatsoever without
written permission except in the case of brief quotations embodied in critical articles
and reviews. For information address HarperCollins Children's Books, a division
of HarperCollins Publishers, 195 Broadway, New York, NY 10007.
www.harpercollinschildrens.com

Library of Congress Control Number: 2022938133
ISBN 978-0-06-306096-8

Typography by Erica De Chavez
22 23 24 25 26 RTLO 10 9 8 7 6 5 4 3 2 1 ❖ First Edition

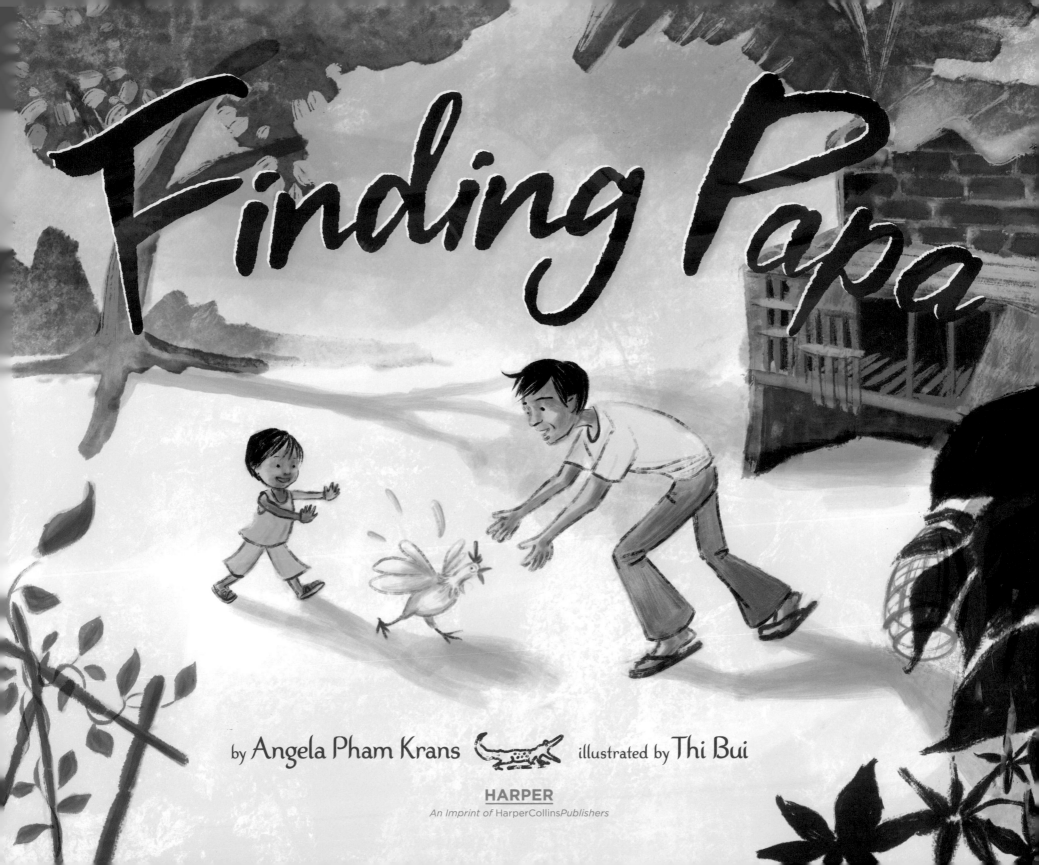

Finding Papa

by Angela Pham Krans   illustrated by Thi Bui

HARPER
An Imprint of HarperCollinsPublishers

Mai's favorite game to play with Papa
was the crocodile chomp. When Papa went

"CHOMP!
CHOMP!"

Mai would giggle and squeal.
Crocodiles were scary, but Papa was not.

One morning, Papa
gave Mai a long hug.

It was longer than usual.

Papa gave Mama a big kiss.

It was bigger than most.

"Goodbye, Papa!"

"Goodbye, Mai!"

Then Mai watched Papa walk down the village dirt road. Papa always waved and smiled at the end of the road, but this time, Papa cried.

Papa did not come home for dinner.

He did not come home for playtime, either.

"Chomp, chomp,"

Mai said to herself.

By bedtime, Mai was crying.
"Where is Papa?"

"Papa is finding a new home
for us." Mama was crying, too.

They hugged each other until they fell asleep.

Mai waited and waited for Papa to come home.
He never arrived, but his letters did. Some were short,
some were long, but Mai and Mama loved them all.

"I want to see Papa again," Mai said.
"Soon, Mai," Mama said.

One night, Mama packed a small bag.

"Where are we going, Mama?"

"We are going to find Papa."

When it was time to leave,
Mai hugged her favorite
mango tree.

She gave her pet
chicken a big kiss.

Then Mai wrapped her arms around Mama's neck and hung on her back.

As Mama walked down the village dirt road, Mai glanced back at her home one last time. "Goodbye," she whispered.

Mama snuck quietly through the
village and around the rice paddies.

The trees shook their branches at Mai.
The tall grass prickled her feet.

Mai and Mama reached the river. As Mama waded through the water, Mai wondered if there were crocodiles nearby.

"Chomp, chomp."

She held Mama tighter.

Mai and Mama finally climbed onto
a boat that was waiting for them.

Mai looked for Papa,
but he was not there.

When Mai awoke, strangers were staring at her. She dug her face into Mama's chest.

"Mama, I'm scared."

"I'm scared, too. Everyone here is looking for their families."

For days, the waves pulled the boat this way. The wind pushed the boat that way. They were surrounded by water, but Mai and Mama had little to drink. At night, Mai's stomach rumbled.

"Chomp, chomp,"

Mai said as she pretended to eat the moon. Mai ached for food and for Papa.

An angry storm came and filled the boat with water.

When a big ship sailed by, everyone
waved their hands and yelled, "Help us!"

The men on the ship lowered a big net down, down, down.

"Climb onto the net," Mama said.

Mai trembled as her feet wobbled with each step. "It's too high up, Mama."

"Be brave, Mai. Climb like you climb your favorite mango tree."

As Mai looked down, it was Mama's turn to climb. Mai yelled as loudly as she could into the wind.

"Be brave, Mama!"

As Mama reached the top, hands stretched out to help her onto the ship.

The ship carried Mai and Mama to a new land where they were surrounded by other people who were rescued from the ocean, too. People in uniform gave them clean water, food, and a place to sleep.

Mai searched for Papa. "Is he here, Mama?"

"No, Mai. Papa was here before us."

Mama lead Mai to a house marked with a number 11 and pointed to the message Papa had left for them.

We will be together soon.
Love,
Papa

Mai believed in Papa's words.
"Chomp, chomp!"
Mai cheered.

Then Mama had an idea.
She shared one of Papa's letters
with a person in uniform.

"We can help you find your Papa,"
he said to Mai.

One day, Mama packed
a small bag again.

"Where are we
going now, Mama?"

"We are going to America."

When Mai and Mama arrived, there were cars going

this way

and

that way.

Through the crowd, Mai saw a man run toward them. Mai did not know this man with a mustache. She grabbed Mama's hand and hid behind her legs.

As he came closer, the man with the mustache crouched on the ground and went,

"CHOMP! CHOMP!"

Mai and Mama giggled.
Crocodiles were scary . . .

But Papa was not.

Author's Note

Finding Papa is based on the real-life journey that my mother and I braved from Vietnam to America in 1983 to reunite with my father. My father had left the country, hoping to find a better opportunity in America to support his family. Along this terrifying journey, we met people who helped us get one step closer to my father. A Nedlloyd Dutch shipping vessel saved my mother and me after we drifted on the ocean for days with little food and drink. The vessel dropped us off at a refugee camp in Singapore, where the American Red Cross helped reunite our family using letters that my father had written to us.

Our family's story is part of a much larger one. When the Vietnam War ended in 1975, thousands of people, referred to as the "boat people," fled the country on boats to escape the political and economic hardships of that time. Their journeys were often met by pirates, storms, and starvation. Some stories ended at sea, while others were the beginning of a new life, but every story is one of unyielding hope and courage.